FEB   2007

The Navajo Year,
Walk Through Many Seasons

Written by Nancy Bo Flood
Illustrated by Billy Whitethorne

Library of Congress Cataloging-in-Publication Data

Flood, Bo.
The Navajo year walk through many seasons / written by Nancy Bo Flood; illustrated by Billy Whitethorne.-- 1st ed.
p. cm.
Summary: Following the Navajo calendar, describes the many sights, sounds, and activities associated with each month.
ISBN 13: 978-1-893354-06-7
ISBN 10: 1-893354-06-7
(hardcover : alk. paper) 1. Navajo calendar--Juvenile literature. 2. Navajo Indians--Rites and ceremonies--Juvenile literature. 3. Navajo Indians--Social life and customs--Juvenile literature. [1. Navajo calendar. 2. Navajo Indians--Social life and customs. 3. Navajo Indians--Folklore. 4. Indians of North America--Arizona--Folklore. 5. Folklore--Arizona.] I. Whitethorne, Billy, ill. II. Title.
E99.N3F57 2006
979.1004'9726--dc22
2005004852

Edited by Jessie Ruffenach
Designed by Bahe Whitethorne, Jr.

Printed in China

First Printing, First Edition
12 11 10 09 08 07 06 10 9 8 7 6 5 4 3 2 1

The paper used in this publication meets the minimum requirements of the American National Standard for Information Sciences — Permanence of Paper for Printed Library Materials, ANSI Z39.48-1984.

Salina Bookshelf, Inc.
Flagstaff, Arizona 86001
www.salinabookshelf.com

For Bill, who has walked with me through many seasons and
For Eva, who begins our family's new season.

-Nancy

In memory of Brian, Melissa, and Audrey
Three inspired people whose work lives on
— Salina Bookshelf

October
Ghąąjį'

Ghąąjį' begins the year,
Separating summer from winter.

The yellow of summer has been walking for six months,
Forward, forward.
Now, at Ghąąjį', yellow summer meets white winter.
Summer stops, goes back. Winter continues on.

"This month is for the people," smiles coyote, "and I shall add one more moon to the year's twelve. This 13th moon belongs to winter if the summer sun has shone too hot. Or this moon belongs to summer if winter's cold needs warming."

Each season must end or the year walks forever forward. The people would not survive.

Coyote smiles again. Good. Now it is Ghąąjį'.

A new year begins.

November

Nílch'ih Ts'ósí

Nílch'ih Ts'ósí brings the slender winds of young winter.

Coyote blinks open his eyes. It is night. The Yei are dancing!
Soon they will be sleeping.

Winter stars are shining. High in the sky in the very middle,
Dilyéhé, the Pleiades, are sparkling bright. These seven star and rainbow children,
the mud people, are circling once again.

Time now for the
Shoe game, string games, sacred tales, and star stories!

Overlooking the hogan but high up on the quiet mesa, coyote curls up tight,
Eyes closed but ears up, listening.
The wind brings Grandfather's voice unraveling an ancient story.

Nítch'ih Tsoh brings whooshing, frost-filled, freezing winds.

The short-light, long-night, cold days of Nítch'ih Tsoh sweep past.

Families – grandmothers and grandfathers, uncles, aunts, and cousins –
Gather for long, night ceremonies. The night air is rich with sounds and smells:
Voices chanting, fires crackling. Mutton stew bubbles and fry bread sizzles.

Br-r-r-r-r, coyote shivers in the great winds, the freezing winds.
"Oh, to be sleeping in a snug, warm hogan!" Coyote shakes off snow and sniffs the
smoke curling up from pine and cedar fires.
"Br-r-r-r-r, the winds keep blowing, blowing, and blowing."

December
Nítch'ih Tsoh

Yas Niłt'ees means carrying buckets of snow to melt into buckets of water.

Then running, sliding, and stomping on mud puddle ice until
Crunch, crackle, splash! Wet feet are freezing.

Around the potbellied stove, children snuggle all wrapped in warm, wool blankets. Red, orange, and purple cocoons wait to feel toasty.
Faces flushed and cheeks soon warm and rosy,
Their fingers fly with string games making Big Star, Many Stars, Lightning and Arrow.
Sh-sh-sh. Spiders and Spider Woman are sleeping.

January
Yas Niłt'ees

February

'Atsá Biyáázh

'Atsá Biyáázh brings the hatching of young eagles.

The days grow longer; the wind blows warmer.
Patches of snow sparkle icy blue back up to a clear, crisp sky.
Frozen waterfalls begin drip, drip, dripping down sheer rock walls.

Sacred stories soon will be put away.

Coyote dozes in the warm, sleepy sun of midday. One eye pops opens.
Shadows criss-cross on the mesa as eagle pairs, male and female, circle overhead.

During Wóózhch'į́į́d, the hungry cries from squawking eaglets echo
Off canyon walls.

Coyote remembers, "I am hungry, too! And soon I'll have lots of hungry little stomachs to feed."

The birthing of lambs begins.
Even the stars are changing.

Coyote growls and howls! "No more strings or stories! Time to prepare for planting!"

Crack! Rumble!
Lightning wakes the holy people,
Thunder bumps, roars, and tumbles.
Clouds open. Rain crashes, splashes.
Dry arroyos swell and swirl.

White winter sighs, stops, and starts walking back . . . back.
Winter ends. A new season begins.

April
T'ą́ą́chil

T'ą́ą́chil brings the first month of summer.
Wild plants appear, shoot up, reach out.
The smallest ones are the first to bloom.

Wild winds of spring whip across the desert.
Whirling, swirling dust devils! Female and male,
Dance, hop, leap
Spinning between mesas.

Parents clean corn planting sticks.
Time to sort seeds, dig holes, then build mounds.
Time to prepare for planting corn, beans, and squash.
The cold walks away.
Warmth returns to the earth.

May

T'ą́ą́tsoh

T'ą́ą́tsoh is the time for being planted, being born.

White faces of calves push and nudge at full udders.
Warm milk drips from their chin whiskers.
Mothers' rough, red tongues scrub skinny sides.
New legs wobble.

In the greening fields, long-legged foals chase each other's shadows until
Yeowwwwww!
Coyote barks!
How they scatter, babies scurrying back to mothers.

June
Ya'iishjááshchilí

Now it is Ya'iishjááshchilí.   The first corn seeds begin growing.

Yucca blossoms open fragrant white mouths.

Green fingers of corn poke through the red earth, reaching up and up
To taste the rain and touch the sun.

Coyote rests atop a butte, watching as the sheep are shorn.
The lambs are bleating.
Yip-yip-yipping! Coyote's pups howl, "Feed me!"

Ya'iishjááshtsoh

Hurry! Ya'iishjááshtsoh is for the planting of late crops!

And the time for
Powwows, rodeos, drumming, bull and bareback riding!
Preparing moccasins, eagle feathers, and beaded bags for dancing.

The people wait for the monsoon rains.

The corn needs rain.
The people need corn: for food, for prayer, for life.

August
Bini'anit'ą́ą́ Ts'ósí

Bini'anit'ą́ą́ Ts'ósí brings long, hot days. Crops ripen.
Beans and corn are ready for harvest.

Pools of purple spread across the desert.
As bee plants burst into bloom,
Their blossoms buzz with visitors.

A yellow blanket of rabbit bush, chamiso, and snakeweed
Spreads across the canyon floor.
Long-eared jack rabbits dodge from coyote's hungry eyes, then
Stand like statues in the shadows.

Yellow-orange buses, red lights flashing,
Gobble up children, then disappear leaving dust puddles.

Bini'anit'ą́ą́ Tsoh

Harvest!

Coyote crosses his paws, rests his chin, and watches. "Good-bye hummingbirds. See you next season."
Toads and lizards, sleepy and sluggish, dig down in the mud, curl under a ledge, and begin winter's long nap.
Juniper berries, pearly purple-white, glow in the moonlight –
As if a thousand spirit eyes were watching.

Coyote gazes at the fat sheep, the round calves, and the piles and piles of
Corn! Stacks of beans! Picked, dried, put away.
"Soon sweet, furry thieves will creep closer and closer to nibble these seeds."
Coyote smacks his lips and grins.

The 13th moon rises round and orange like a full, fat stomach filled with corn.
Yellow summer stops. Steps back.

White winter walks forward . . . forward . . . and
A new month, a new cycle,
A new year begins.